Over the gate
at number 8,
round the back,
through the flap
and onto the lap
of...

HODDER CHILDREN'S BOOKS

First published in Great Britain
in 2018 by Hodder and Stoughton

Copyright © Chloë and Mick Inkpen, 2018

Hodder Children's Books
An imprint of Hachette Children's Group
Part of Hodder and Stoughton
Carmelite House
50 Victoria Embankment
London, EC4Y 0DZ

A CIP catalogue record for this book is
available from the British Library.

ISBN 978 1 444 94009 1

1 3 5 7 9 10 8 6 4 2

Printed in China

An Hachette UK Company
www.hachette.co.uk
www.hachettechildrens.co.uk

Mrs Blackhat

Chloë and Mick Inkpen

Hodder
Children's
Books

Black boots
　　black gloves
black hair
　　black hat
black wand
black chair
　　black broom
black mat
　　black crow
black bat
　　black toad
black rat

everything black
everything black
　　everything black

except for the cat . . .

...which is
ginger!

'Ginger cat? Ginger cat?'
says Mrs Blackhat.
'We'll see about that!'

'Aha, just the thing!'
Her laptop goes . . . ping!

And in no time at all
the doorbell goes . . .

ding!

Inky stinkle
starry twinkle
squiddy ink
and raven's back,
toady nosewarts
Liquorice Allsorts
thunder cloud
and thunder crack.

Make this ginger cat
turn black!

But the cat . . .
the cat . . .
the cat . . .

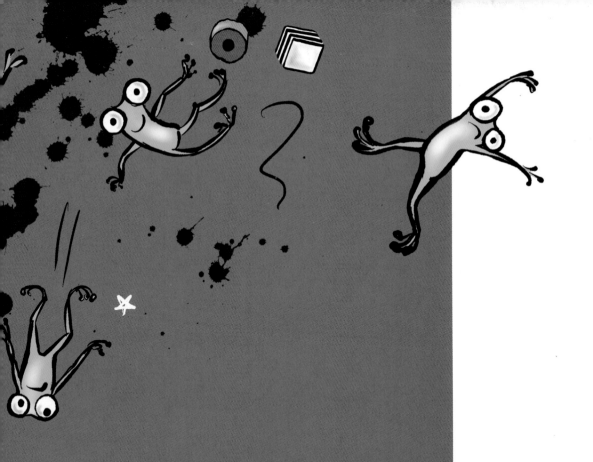

...is still
ginger!

Back on the laptop
clickety clack!
'What else can I buy
to turn my cat black?'

'Aha! Very nice!
And only half price!
A bargain at 4.94!
Just the thing for my spell.
It will do very well.'
And soon there's a ring
at the door.

Stinky pinky purple stuff.
Seven drops is just enough.

Three steps forward.
Three steps back.
Three steps sideways.
Raise your hat.

Wave your wand and
Whack! Whack! Whack!
Make this ginger cat
turn black!

But the cat...
the cat...
the cat...

. . . is still ginger

. . . still ginger

. . .still annoyingly ginger.

Back on the laptop,
Ping! Ping! Ping!
Wearing out the doorbell!
Ding! Dong! Ding!

Ding! Dong!

Ding! Dong!

No more shopping!
Not another thing!
What a load of rubbish!
Chuck it in the bin!
Please don't send me
any more stuff!
Goodbye Shopalot!
I've had enough!

One week later . . .

Ding! Dong! Ding!

What on earth is that!
I didn't order anything!

And soon, that
very afternoon...

Hubble bubble
toilet trouble!
Quake and shake and
creak and crack!
Fire burn and
cauldron wobble,
make this ginger cat

turn black!

Shiver, quiver,

judder, shudder,

grumble, rumble...

all stand back!

Now nothing,
no nothing,
no **nothing** is black!

Not the crow,
not the bat,
not the toad,
not the rat.
Not the wand,
not the chair,
not the broom,
not the mat.
Not the boots,
not the gloves,
not the hair,
nor the hat.

And the cat?
And the cat?
And the cat . . .

. . .well the stripes on a **tiger** are black!

And the cat?
   And the cat?
And the cat . . .

...well the stripes on a **tiger** are black!

'And I **like** it
like that!'
says Mrs Blackhat.